THIS BECCA'S BUNCH BOOK BELONGS TO

. . . .

. . . .

EGMONT

We bring stories to life

First Published in Great Britain 2020 by Egmont UK Limited

2 Minster Court, 10th floor, London EC3R 7BB

www.egmont.co.uk

Written by Jude Exley

Designed by Kelly-Anne Levey

The Wagtastic Four is based on a television script written by P. Kevin Strader and Sarah Jenkins

Becca's Bunch is produced by Jam Media

Created by Chris Dicker and Conor Finnegan

ISBN 978 1 4052 9667 0

70811/001

Printed in Poland

THE
WAGTASTIC
FOUR

One morning in Wagtail Woods, Pops was reading Becca her favourite book.

"The **superhero** saved the day!" read Pops. "Everyone cheered,

'**Tweet, tweet, hooray!**'"

"That's so cool, Pops," said Becca. "I'd love to be a superhero."

She thought for a minute. "Hey, maybe the Bunch could be superheroes with me? We could go on **super special missions!**"

"I'm on my way!" said Sylvia.

Russell wasn't sure whether Becca had said **super** or **supper**. "Either way, I'm there!" he said.

Becca read the story to the Bunch. Everyone wanted to be a **superhero!**

"I hope there's some **exciting adventures** out there for us today," said Russell.

"But not **too scary**," added Pedro.

They needed costumes, so Becca dragged the dressing up box to the centre of the Clubhouse.

"Let's dress for action!" she said.

Wagtail Woods was about to get its very own superheroes: **The Wagtastic Four.**

"Adventure's Calling!" chirped Becca.

The Wagtastic Four bounded into the woods, ready for action.

"**Let's wing it!**" said Becca.

They saw Uncle Ned in his garden. Someone to help! But before they could help him water his plants, the **supervillains** Baddy Badger and the Rotten Carrots showed up!

"**Prickly pinecones!** We have villains on our hands," cried Becca.

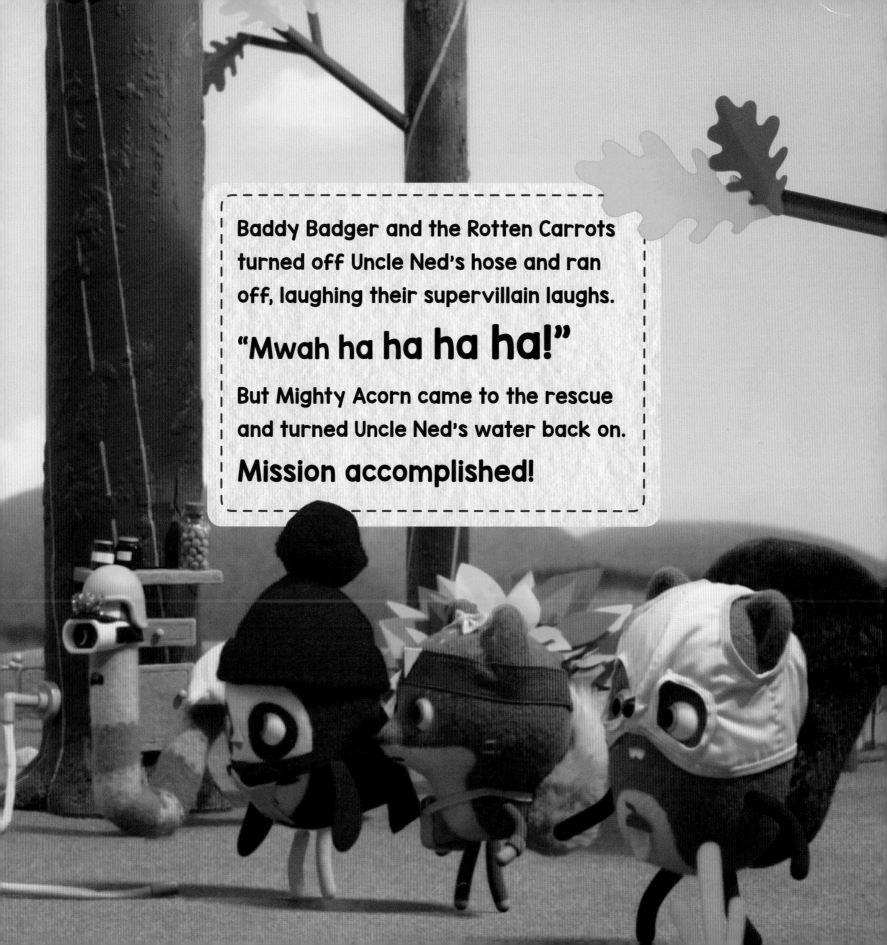

Baddy Badger and the Rotten Carrots turned off Uncle Ned's hose and ran off, laughing their supervillain laughs.

"Mwah ha ha ha ha!"

But Mighty Acorn came to the rescue and turned Uncle Ned's water back on.

Mission accomplished!

In town, the Wagtastic Four saw Baddy Badger and the Rotten Carrots take one of postmoose MJ's letters with a fishing rod.

"Fear not, MJ!" declared Becca. And Ultimate Bag Girl's trusty scissors cut the fishing line and retrieved the letter!

"Macadamia!" cheered Russell. "We're going to have **another exciting adventure** soon," said Becca. "I can feel it in my wings."

Suddenly, the Wagtastic Four heard something. Was it someone needing to be rescued?

They rushed into the woods and found little Barry swinging on the tyre swing.

"I'm a **superhero** too and I'm **flying!**" said Barry. "Push me higher!"

"I think you're swinging high enough, little guy," said Becca.

But the Rotten Carrots had heard Barry, too. **"We'll push you**, Barry," said Baddy Badger and she gave the swing a really big push.

The tyre swing went **up, up, up** ...

And then it came back down – **without Barry!**

Everyone looked up.

Barry waved from high up in the tree.

The tyre swing swung down again. This time it grabbed Baddy Badger and the Rotten Carrots and swept them up. Now they were stuck in the tree too! **"HELP!"** they cried.

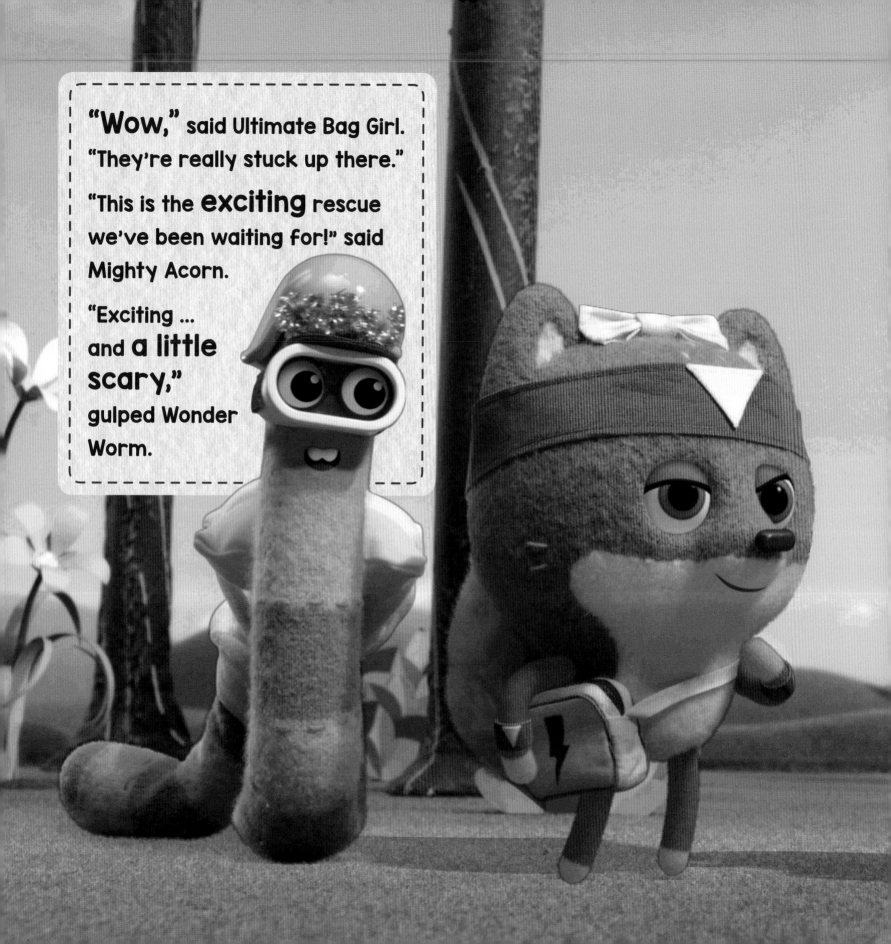

"**Wow**," said Ultimate Bag Girl. "They're really stuck up there."

"This is the **exciting** rescue we've been waiting for!" said Mighty Acorn.

"Exciting ... and **a little scary**," gulped Wonder Worm.

The Wagtastic Four gathered in a circle.
"I have an idea!" said Superbird.

"A zipline!" cried Superbird.
"Helmets on, everyone."

With that, Baddy Badger, Barry and The Rotten Carrots began their slide.

Ahhhhhhhhh!

Very soon, everyone was safely on the ground.
The Wagtastic Four had saved the day!

"Well, we **didn't really** need saving," said Beatrice.

"**Nope**," said Casper.

"**Not us**," said Jasper.

"Yes, you did!" said Barry. "Remember? Help!"

"OK, OK, we did need help," said Beatrice.

"Thanks for saving us Wagtastic Four."

"All's good in the wood!" said Becca.

"Super good! Tweet, tweet,

hooray!"